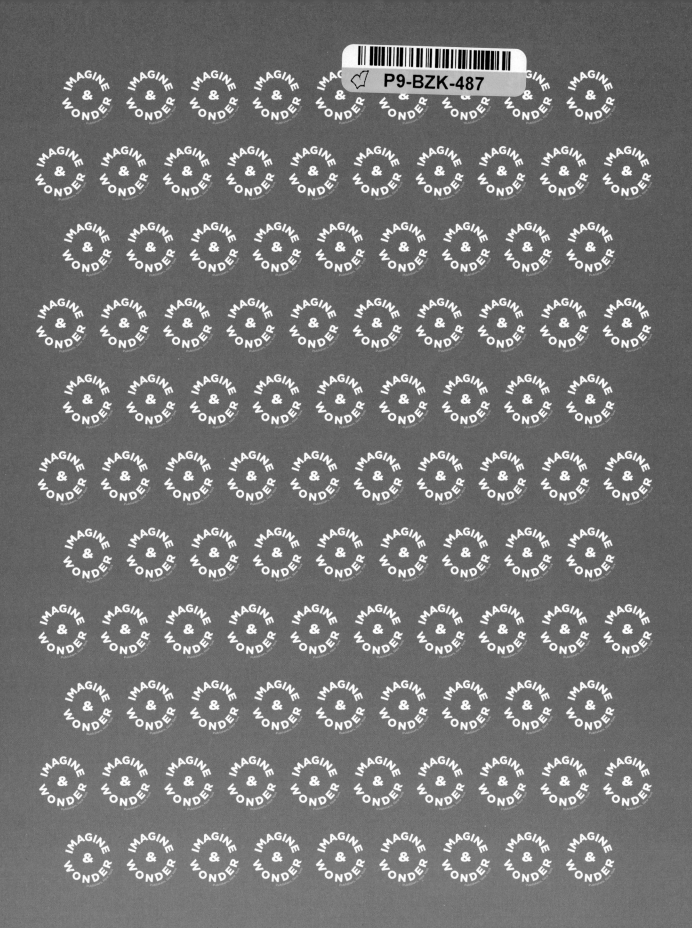

IMAGINE & WONDER
Publishers, New York

THURMAN GOES GREEN

A Turtle's Guide for a Cleaner Planet

by Artie Knapp

Illustrated by
MJ Illustrations

IMAGINE
&
WONDER™
Publishers, New York

EVERYONE HAD GATHERED for the big day. The wedding of Miss Taylor Turtley was an event that every turtle within a hundred yards vowed not to miss.

Everything had seemed perfect, too, but then it happened! Litter suddenly blanketed the wedding party — even the bride and groom!

Bags of trash had been thrown from the overpass that towered over the creek.

But such behavior was no longer going to be tolerated — at least not by Taylor's brother Thurman.

As Thurman glanced over at his sister, who was in tears, banana peels covered her wedding dress and shell.

"That's it! Enough is enough!" exclaimed Thurman with his fist aimed high.

"Forget it, Thurman," said his father. "There's nothing we can do about the humans, Son."

"Forget it? How can you say that, Dad? Something has to be done. It's time for action!" Thurman said.

And with that, Thurman told everyone he had to go.

"Where are you going, Thurman?" asked his mother.

"I'm going to put a stop to this, Mom."

"Don't go!" shouted a voice from the wedding party.

"You'll end up in a kid's fish bowl, and you'll barely have room to stretch!"

"You'll be soup, Thurman!" shouted another.

As voices continued to ring out about the dangers that awaited him, Thurman was undeterred. He was determined to make a difference.

How exactly? Well, Thurman wasn't sure. He just knew he couldn't sit by as the land he loved became cluttered with trash.

Traveling a distance of any length takes quite a while for a turtle. So, to make headway on his journey, Thurman swam with the current of a nearby river.

After a couple of days adrift, Thurman finally saw signs of human civilization. And everywhere he looked there was trash—lots, and lots of trash.

Dumping garbage where they didn't live was bad enough, but Thurman was surprised to see people living in it.

There was garbage in their water. It littered the streets where they drove their automobiles and it was even where children played.

As Thurman pondered how he was going to address the crisis, several people were suddenly approaching him.

Fearing for his safety, he quickly turned to hide; and then everything turned dark. Thurman had stuck his head into a muddied plastic bottle that had been left on the riverbed. Eager to escape, he pulled with all of his might, but without success.

A science teacher from a nearby elementary school was now standing close to the river with her students. They were on a field trip to help the environment. The children would be planting trees, and a local newspaper reporter was on hand to cover the event.

"Okay, before we get started, who knows the answer?" asked Mrs. Thornberry.

Several of the students raised their hands. "Yes, Susie," said Mrs. Thornberry.

"It's our carbon footprint," said the young girl.

"That's right, Susie. Very good! Even though each and every one of us has our own carbon footprint, it affects everyone and everything around us."

As her students began breaking ground to plant trees, Mrs. Thornberry continued to speak about the different effects that carbon footprints have on the environment.

She reminded the children of the pollution that comes from factories and automobiles, and the carbon dioxide that is released into the air because of them.

By planting trees that day, the children would be combating carbon dioxide by putting more oxygen back in the air.

"Does everyone remember the four Rs that we discussed in class?" asked Mrs. Thornberry.

"Yes, Mrs. Thornberry," said her students in unison. "Rethink, Reduce, Reuse," but then young Robby Pursley shouted, "Recycle," before any of the other students could say the last word.

You see, Robby couldn't contain his excitement. He had stumbled across a plastic bottle. But it was no ordinary bottle. It had a turtle stuck in it.

As everyone came over to view the bottle, Robby held it up in the air for all to see. The local news reporter captured the moment with his camera.

As Thurman began to feel his body being tugged, he feared the worst. Then suddenly, the brightness of the sun shone over him!

"Wow! Look at him," said Robby.

One by one the students touched Thurman's shell. Even through his fear, Thurman felt comforted when hearing what the children were doing for the environment.

The anger that had driven him to leave his home suddenly faded away. Because of the actions of the children that day, Thurman knew there was hope for a cleaner world.

"Can I keep him, Mrs. Thornberry?"

"I don't think that is a good idea, Robby. This is his home. He needs to be set free."

Robby sighed but did as his teacher requested. He wiped the mud off Thurman's shell and released him.

After he had finally reached home, Thurman was greeted as a hero. He learned that his rescue had made the front page of the local newspaper.

Inspired by the story, every school in the region began cleaning up the trash that littered the area, to include rivers and ponds.

Thurman just didn't understand why everyone back home made such a big fuss. Besides, there was much work to do, and getting stuck in a bottle wasn't exactly what he had planned.

But Thurman's family reminded him of the courage it took to do what he did. His quest for change was proof that one individual can make a difference, and that each and every one of us should try.

"It's up to you!"

For Alanna, Love Dad

AK

Thurman Goes Green
A Turtle's Guide for a Cleaner Planet
Story by Artie Knapp
© Copyright 2021

Thurman Goes Green: A Turtle's Guide for a Cleaner Planet
1st Edition
© Copyright 2021, Imagine & Wonder, Publishers, New York
All rights reserved. www.imagineandwonder.com
Library of Congress Control Number: 2021933146
ISBN: 9781953652843

Scan the QR code with your phone camera to find more titles like this
from Imagine and Wonder

Your guarantee of quality
As publishers, we strive to produce every book to the highest commercial standards. The printing and binding have been planned to ensure a sturdy, attractive publication which should give years of enjoyment. If your copy fails to meet our high standards, please inform us and we will gladly replace it.

Printed in China by Hung Hing Off-set Printing Co. Ltd.

Scan the QR code to find other
amazing adventures and more from
www.ImagineAndWonder.com

IMAGINE & WONDER
Publishers, New York